D0388678

# THE IMMORTALS

SUNY SERIES, AFRO-LATINX FUTURES   *Vanessa K. Valdés, editor*

MAKENZY ORCEL

# THE IMMORTALS

*Translated from the French by Nathan H. Dize*

Original title: Les Immortelles

Copyright: © Mémoire d'encrier, 2010.
© 2020 State University of New York

Published by arrangement with Éditions Zulma, Paris.

Published by State University of New York Press, Albany

All rights reserved

Printed in the United States of America

No part of this book may be used or reproduced in any manner whatso-
ever without written permission. No part of this book may be stored in
a retrieval system or transmitted in any form or by any means including
electronic, electrostatic, magnetic tape, mechanical, photocopying,
recording, or otherwise without the prior permission in writing of
the publisher.

For information, contact State University of New York Press,
Albany, NY
www.sunypress.edu

**Library of Congress Cataloging-in-Publication Data**
Names: Orcel, Makenzy, 1983- author. | Dize, Nathan H.,
    1989- translator.
Title: The immortals / Makenzy Orcel, translated from the French by
    Nathan H. Dize.
Other titles: Immortelles. English
Description: Albany : State University of New York Press, [2020] |
    Series: SUNY series, Afro-Latinx futures | Translated into English
    from French.
Identifiers: LCCN 2019058551 | ISBN 9781438480565 (paperback) |
    ISBN 9781438480572 (ebook)
Subjects: LCSH: Haiti Earthquake, Haiti, 2010—Fiction.
Classification: LCC PQ3949.3.O72 I4613 2020 | DDC 843/.92—dc23
LC record available at https://lccn.loc.gov/2019058551

10  9  8  7  6  5  4  3  2  1

*Without knowing why*
*I love this world*
*Where we come to die*
NATSUME SŌSEKI

*To all the whores of Grand Rue*
*Taken by the violent earthquake January 12, 2010.*

*To Grisélidis Réal.*

# CONTENTS

*All the cries of the earth echo in my belly.*

My name is . . . Actually, my name doesn't matter. The whores, they don't give a fuck if you're a writer or anything else. You pay them. They make you come. And you get the hell out after. Just like nothing happened. For the rest of us, the clients, it's the same: our names don't matter. It's like going all over the place shouting that the world is round. That God exists. And yet, the earth has never been as round as the existence of God. . . . "I'm a writer." That's what I tell them when people ask me what I do for a living. An affirmation that somehow for me rings false, since I write with death and in death. This place escapes weight-iness. Escapes time-space. Between elsewhere and childhood. The moment when *this thing* happened, I was rereading *Les Fleurs du mal*. Baudelaire is a real bird of ill omens. He always comes with death on the tip of his beak. The last time, it was a violent nervous breakdown. I only just barely snapped out of it. She seemed to have understood the power of writing by asking me to write this book about Grand Rue. For all of the other whores that disappeared in *this thing*. A book, she said, to make them living, immortal. She told me her story. I only had to transform it. Find the correct formulation to explain her pain, her memories, her anxieties and everything else . . . To write with another at the helm. With her tears, her silence trailing each word. Each parcel of unknown earth, unnavigable . . . Taken by the strip-tease of death. What had Grand Rue had become. Port-au-Prince. The city where I grew up. The city of my first poems. I wasn't sure that I could make it. For me, sex and alcohol were the best therapy. I ran from everything, even writing. I mean, I didn't want to write immediately, at least I

~1~

thought it wasn't possible. . . . Swimming in whiskey, I slid into the infamous landscape of this room that stank of shit and death and drowned myself in its ocean of whores. It's the first time that I entered a whorehouse with an *a priori* as egotistical as the pleasure of floating amongst the stars. . . . She lit a cigarette, took a long drag and let escape a thick cloud of smoke from her mouth, and then from her nose. To me, she looked phenomenal with her whorish wiles.

—So, what do you do for a living?

My favorite question.

—I'm a writer.

—A writer! That works out great. . . . You give me what I ask you for and after you can have me in any way you desire.

Deal. I first just had to write and then fuck her. This idea was rather pleasing to me. After all, books don't sell so well. Writing for sex. That could compensate certain things. She moved toward the window to contemplate, not without bitterness, the immense valley of concrete and white dust outside. The irreparable. The ineffable. The despair that flowed from people's eyes. The city of rubble, shredded, saturated in identifiable, unidentifiable, and synthesized dead people, creating all sorts of geometric figures. Then suddenly, like that, improvising like a punch to the mouth, she let loose a sentence that swept away the silence: "The little girl. She's still stuck under the rubble, twelve days after having prayed to all of the saints . . ."

The time has now come to go searching for her treasure. I have nothing more to do here. I owe her at least that much, after all that we've been through together. It's the only way for me to redeem myself for having offered her a place on my raft drifting away aimlessly. These frenzies that have over time worn away my youth. Into an empty calabash. I'm going to leave to find what meant the most to her in all her fucking life. Her son. But before, I want to recount. Let the blood flow from my words. Recount. Redemption. If only it were so simple.

The little girl. She was dead after twelve days under the rubble, after having prayed to all of the saints. That night, the earth drifted. Fluttered. Danced. Self-harmed in order to exhume itself from within. Tore itself apart. Laid on the ground like the dead. Traipsing over its own wreckage.

I still remember the day where she broke all the bonds between us and ran off with this man, this so-called professor of literature. She hated that we interfered in her personal affairs. Did she also prefer to be elsewhere the whole day so to not have to put up with my frequent nervous breakdowns . . . Useless to dig up old bones now. Let's begin. I'll talk. You, the writer, you write. You transform. The others always begin with prayer. I want us to begin with poetry. She loved poetry.

*And I who was time*
*Space, the crossing*
*The beginning and the end*
*The splendors of the world*
*All the cries of the earth*
*Echo in my belly*


—Not bad, writer. It looks like you're reading the depths of my soul.

In the end, a male poet is a little bit like a woman knocked up by words.

The Red BMW Man never washes himself. I realized it from the smell of herring he gave off. I feel on the verge of tears when my body beneath him acts as a site of mystery and redemption. I dream of being one of these children who aren't yet aware of their actions. These children that I have left unborn out of selfishness. Out of a love for starkness. He reeks, certainly, but he is generous, always giving into my whims as a woman for sale, as a woman with fluvial expectations.

My name is … Actually, my name doesn't matter. My name is the last piece of intimacy I have left. The clients don't really give a fuck. They pay. I make them come. And they leave like it was nothing. That's all.

The little girl. I'm the one who taught her all she knows about the profession and the street.

—We're insignificant, on the order of mirages. Your body is your sole instrument, little girl.

Yet, I was only ashamed by the idea that this single window was the only viable part, the only part capable of putting me up for sale.

Nothing was like it was before. Before, I thought that each pass-erby was a star, capable of making me forget once and for all. To forget that I am a part of a long line of whores, that I am myself a whore, that my future depends on it. To forget her voice beneath the rubble, a broken voice calling for help. Shit, how to forget?

The little girl. When she jumped on board the irreversible she was at the age where words hesitate. Wet, furtive words, not of any language, rather that of the *sine qua non*. An obligatory journey. Twelve years in the face of night. Free to be alone, whatever she wanted. Twelve years becoming herself.

The words, my love, are the lairs of blood and screams. I'm telling this for you, my little girl. I'm telling you and calling you from my internal exile. From my most secret, most distant island. The words, my love, are silent. My gestures also name you. All of my body's words could not suffice to tell you the earth's pain.

Everyone spoke of the end of time or of the end of the world. Me, I thought of the little girl; I don't know what the end of time or the end of the world is like, nor the end of anything. It's always after the rain, comes the sun. The sea is blue. The girls are pretty. The dogs bark. The passersby pass and pass. Where to? I still hear their mumbling, the breath of these filthy beasts, thirsting for depth. These passersby, these beasts who once thought themselves to be human.

Everything began in her eyes many days before. Just after this dream that she refused to tell. It wasn't yet the end, in the first seconds. Something had just slipped beneath our feet, defying the imperialism of our joy. It was brief.

The little girl. She was the first to scream. The last one also to pass away. After twelve days. After having prayed to all of the saints. She, as frail as she was, spent many days stuck beneath all that men consider the mark of greatness, of social mobility.

Me? Understand? I only asked you to write, to play your role as a writer while I speak. How dare you ask me that? Poetry isn't supposed to understand. Only to feel. To feel until you cry or vomit. Sometimes she cried after reading your nonsense. I never asked myself the reason why this taxi driver payed me twice what he earned during the day for twelve years just so that he could sleep in my bed. Without touching me once. How do you expect me to understand what happened that night?

The little girl. She had the ability to see the future in her dreams. If she told you that the street will be dirty at twelve twenty-six and ten seconds and that two people will lose their lives, it's sure to happen. And she can recall everything in strong detail. She can even tell you their sort, the exact place where these people will die like dogs. We say that the street is dirty when the big bad bandits come out of their lairs to sow trouble. To reign supreme streets over the streets with impunity. To make bullets sing. To quench their thirst for blood. Each time we asked her to recall her dream, she said it was nothing. But her eyes had already deceived her. Her eyes too full of sorrow to not announce a misfortune so close in proximity. Speaking of misfortune, why does the image of the taxi driver come to me all of the sudden?

That day, the bedroom still reeked from the passage of clients. Here, a sort of disorder reigned that felt irreparable. She spent the whole day on the moon, in her fucking novels. She's like that, the little girl. There are those days where she's a machine, she can do it all. And others where she rejects everything and plunges into her books. Where she scorns everything. But this time, it had nothing to do with her dirty feet or a client's bad breath or an accidently broken nail. She just said that she had a dream that could not be told.

The Red BMW Man is quite different from the others. When he takes possession of me—one might say he is like a ferocious beast that hasn't eaten for an eternity and had found a rotting carcass in the road—my belly responds like the epicenter of a violent earthquake. I ask myself how a human being can have such an enormous member and have such a foul stench.

With time, I learned to get used to his member and his stench. In this country you must set your priorities, identify what is indispensable to your life, or rather, to your survival. In my profession, you can't waste time being picky, weighing the consequences, choosing. You don't know how to choose when you're paid to dole out pleasure. To suck and suck some more without the right to have had enough, to no longer want anymore. To be treated like a dog. But when it comes to these tiny details, this man takes pity. He's too vulnerable. Like the targets that are constantly caught in the crosshairs of others. And we've hardly started on him. We say that he looks like one of those stupid animals that enjoys itself bouncing from branch to branch eating bananas all the livelong day. That he walks with his ass clamped shut like a dog on the verge of shitting. But I like him fine. He's my animal. I want to have him all. But he pays me. For example, to smack my ass when he fucks me.

—Shake that thing!

The little girl. She shouldn't have taken cover inside that half-dozen story monster. She dishonored me. As well as all the other immortals of Grand Rue. The street had always been our only shelter, our only place to be among everyone else . . . I must ask you, writer, to remove that part. It feels like it's already been said, recycled. But, don't we also write with the words of others?

No, she shouldn't have preferred that concrete monster to our little end of the street because she didn't understand at all what was happening, never heard about it, never saw trembling earth unleash itself, rippling like a dugout canoe on a stormy sea; even the spirited reader of Jacques Stephen Alexis that she was.

~

How would you like me, writer, to understand what happened that night? There was a minute, what am I saying, a few seconds that she was there, still dreaming, talking about treasure and planned to put some money to the side to go on her search. It wasn't until the same day as the drama that I understood the treasure was her son. After thirty-five seconds, the monster fell. And it was truly the end.

Go fuck yourself, Jacques Stephen Alexis! Everyone says that you're such a great writer, and your books can't even teach one of your faithful readers what an earthquake is. How to react when one occurs. What is the point of even being a writer? She died because of you. Because your words were incapable of saving her.

Fedna, when it comes to blowjobs that girl is a genius. You'd have to be a real cheat not to give her a little gratification after her performance. "God gave us a mouth to suck with, right?" She said. We called her Fedna "The Blowjob Queen." She knew from the first tremors that it was an earthquake. She had without a doubt already seen one on TV. But she didn't know how to escape. She was too crazy about TV. She ate with the TV on. She put on make-up with the TV on. Threw her legs into the air with the TV on. Actually, she did everything with the TV on. I remember one time. At the time I didn't live in this room, where I take my clients. I tricked at Drôle-de-fesses. The oldest whorehouse on Grand Rue. I was servicing the Red BMW Man at the time. I heard her, from the other side of the dirty sheet that separated our beds, pressuring her client to come. That's all she loves, Fedna. The TV. Those Latin American soap operas that come on in the late afternoon. I surprised myself watching them attentively from time to time, with their saccharine childishness. But not to the point of rushing a client. Or of closing my ears to the calling of a friend.

The TV took its time explaining to Fedna "The Blowjob Queen" what an earthquake was. In the end, she wasn't able to escape. She was flattened along with her armchair by the concrete ceiling.

The TV had many versions of the thing, just like every other event it discusses. First, it said that the earthquake was the manifestation of God's anger in the face of disobedience, criminality, and human debauchery. Next, that it was our heroes of independence expressing their displeasure with what we've done to the country. Then it slipped into idle gossip, enumerating the number of countries that have experienced earthquakes that lasted about as long as a fart, an ejaculation, the creaking of a door as it slowly opens, very slowly, to let the silence in, by citing statistics that have nothing to do with reality. The TV spoke of different types of plates, the activity of fault lines, the earth's crust and all that.

It's strange. You finally find someone you get along with, someone with whom you can share everything. Then, one day, like that, they leave forever. Without the slightest chance that you'll see them again. And this, in no other life. I'm sick of this shit. About karma, about reincarnation, about metempsychosis, etc. To me all of that is a bunch of bullshit. That nobody will come tell me that we had lives before that, and that we'd have another one after and after. I'm only concerned about the one that I have right now, the one that beats in my chest, courses through my veins, trying to live life to the fullest. Fucking period.

To my mother, when you die, you get to join those who left a long time ago. To my grandfather, a former tax collector and relentless liver of the fast life, you dance Carnival in another life. Go and meet the little girl. Dance Carnival. Or simply depart just because I must. Because I have nothing left to do here. It's the most beautiful dream that I ever had.

The little girl. Her death left me with a great void. An irreparable void, I'd even say. All these sandwiched bodies, dislocated between the loose masses of reinforced concrete. All these screams calling for Jesus. It's the first time I've heard so many people asking for Jesus. That I ever saw so many arms reaching for the heavens.

Jesus, for many people—especially Christians—was both the author of *this thing* and the savior of all of those who escaped unharmed. A woman who just emerged from the rubble waved her arms in the air and began to shout all around her: *men Jezi m t ap pale w la*. Here's the Jesus I was telling you about. When he's your one and only savior, this is what he's capable of. A thousand houses fall down to your left. A thousand fall to your right. You will not be trapped. Hallelujah! After all, *this thing* was the only trophy Jesus had left to win to be considered the greatest champion of all time, to become unquestionably, indubitably the most murderous and ridiculed dead person of all time.

Her mother. She lived in Martissant and sold bibles and books of Gospel songs. This poor woman would have given everything to see her daughter succeed. As long as her daughter was exactly like her. Christian, pretentious, hostile towards everything of this earth. Sometimes nature works against itself. There's nothing you can do.

The little girl had always been so ironic. It was undoubtedly thanks to those books that she never ceased to devour day in and day out. How could she love me, me? Nobody had ever told me such a thing before. That's what she told me when it was all over.

Did she know that she was going to die? Had she already seen it in her dreams, that she would end up like that, stuck in a corner under the rubble from which nobody could pull her out. Even the White aid-workers. Even their highly trained dogs, more intelligent, more well-kept than the *ti nèg*\* from here.

---

\* *Ti nèg* is a Haitian Creole euphemism for people of modest social or socioeconomic backgrounds. It frequently carries an element of contempt when used, especially when used to distinguish between the wealthy (*gwo nèg*) and the poor (*ti nèg*).

The little girl. She isn't dead. She doesn't have the right to die. I still smell her odor in everything that moves. It's the odor of catastrophe, the odor of the cadavers mounting from the street, the odor of everything that moves. All the concrete monsters have fallen. All the brothels. Grand Rue isn't what it used to be. But us, we'll never die. We, the whores of Grand Rue. We are the immortals.

Contrary to her mother's wishes, she loved everything that was of this world, because this world, she said, is where the street was and in the street the wind, the freedom to never stop. She was known as Shakira, like the celebrity. She was a great reader of Jacques Stephen Alexis, the famous Haitian writer who disappeared under François Duvalier's dictatorship. Nobody could keep her from being simultaneously the echo and the contradiction of herself. Nobody.

The little girl. She shouldn't have been there, in this place, at this exact moment when *this thing* happened. She'd planned to go visit Emma, a fellow streetwalker who was ill. If she hadn't changed her mind, maybe the end would've been different. If only I hadn't forced her to put away her books, to walk the streets and stir up more clients.

No, she shouldn't have told me that she had a son somewhere, abandoned in the immense swamp that is the world. Sometimes it's urgent, she said, to let everything go, to abandon everything, even what is most dear, all to pursue your dreams. . . . She shouldn't have told me that she was counting on me to find him, her son. That she loved me. That she appreciated all that I had done for her. It was to tell me how self-centered and insensitive I was to have offered her the street, this shitty profession. But what else did I have to offer her? Can you offer what you don't have? Why did she pass over all the doors of Grand Rue, all the doors in the world, to come knock at mine?

Poor Emma. She suffered from this illness that I don't want to mention here so as to not worry those who have already been on the other side of her little panties. . . . Before, she worked as a maid in one of those great big bourgeois houses in the hills. One day, she ran away after poking out her boss's eye, the one who wanted, above all else, to have sex with her without her consent. Those versed in the art of gossip say that the boss's wife found her stealing her jewelry or sucking off her husband; everything depends on the version the story and who is doing the telling. They would've thrown her out the door like a stray bitch. Géralda Huge-Tits introduced her to El Caucho the Cuban. The manager of Drôle-de-fesses who employed her without any questions asked. Drôle-de-fesses, I'll remind you, is the brothel where I used to work. Well before I moved into this room from which I'm telling this story so that you, the writer, can turn it into a book, so that you immortalize all the whores of Grand Rue, taken away by *this thing*. Emma's body was never recovered.

I know by heart all of the nooks and crannies of this concrete desert. All the faces. All the whims of the clientele. The city is a sad painting where animals and humans eat from and do their business on the same plate. Quite the match.

Grand Rue, it wasn't just the street intersected by a thousand other streets, the bastion of cheap sex. Flocks of whores lined up on the sidewalks at all hours of the day. The rotten sheets, pinned to the balconies flutter in the wind, giving the buildings wings, making them look like large immobile birds. But also, the eruption of a whole world that jumps out before your eyes. Walking market women who harass the passersby. Panicked passersby in the midst of an auditory assault by the jerry-rigged pick-up trucks smeared with naive paintings. Hordes of the famished, of thieves who steal the wallets of distracted and reckless passersby. The police who track them like dogs. Stinking dogs. The shit. The mountains of trash. The sidewalks bursting with people. The insane. The homeless. The interminable honking of cars caught in traffic jams. The children of streets turned into improvised carwashes. The wads of dollars exhibited by the foreign exchange dealers. It was also this, Grand Rue. More than this.

My grandmother, my mother, my aunts, my cousins (all whores as well), they told me about this Port-au-Prince of old. The streets were clean and the men respected ladies. A time when an all-inclusive session between the sheets was worth no more than twelve *goud*. A time when they hadn't quite started this seaside Venice of fortune that it has become today by pushing away the water to plant houses that, with time, sink into the earth and others that haphazardly crawl up into the mountains like children scribbling with crayons. It's a moment in time that I never knew. I came into this world too late.

May I continue. . . ? Have you taken note of everything, writer, all the silences, everything left unsaid. . . ? It's been twelve years—it's the mother who's talking now—since my daughter left home. Since she's been gone. My greatest worry is that I will get to the point where I won't be able to do anything. To continue looking for her. To fight. I know that this day will come. It'll come. And I'll kill myself to put an end to all of this.

The little girl. Already twelve years since she left her mother's house to become the most beautiful, coveted whore of Grand Rue. Twelve years without a word. Twelve years of silence. It was her fault that she left. It was your fault that she left because you did nothing to keep her there, you piece of shit mother!

Her mother. She was actually quite a marvelous woman. A woman who wanted the best for her child. For her to be different. To see differently what all the others see with ordinary eyes. Never allowing her to identify with these vain models on magazine covers. She never hesitated to go to bed hungry. She destroyed herself for her daughter's well-being. And she wasn't ready to see her leave like that in a cloud of smoke for all these years of sustained fighting against death.

What wouldn't this woman do to be reunited with her daughter? She looked and looked for her constantly, for twelve long years, looking for at least a trace of life. After *this thing*, was it necessary to continue looking for someone who never came home? I don't believe in miracles.

My daughter—desperate, it's still the mother talking—it's best for you to go even farther away. Far away from home. As far as possible. So that you forget me completely instead of being little more than a heap of bloody flesh stuck under the rubble. At least there will be a survivor, somewhere, who forgets the existence of her poor mother.

Misfortunes—can they compare to one another? Do they shrink to the point of disappearing, to the point of being locked away? Are there some that are more insignificant or profound than others? When this passerby told me about what she was going through, of her misfortune, I felt a certain discomfort regarding the disappearance of my daughter. It seemed like a drop of water in the ocean. She lost her husband, her sister, her older brother, her two cousins, her two sons, her youngest daughter, the first son's girlfriend, the wife of one of her two cousins, her house, her dog. In the end, *this thing* took everything from her. Me too, my daughter.

No, I don't want to forget. Forgetting is the worst kind of catastrophe. It's the first time in my life that I saw the wound from so close, the vulnerabilities of the world with so much pathos, real pathos. That I've seen everyone crying, all at once. Everyone. Without exception.

I'm the one who taught her everything about the profession and about the street, at least my own philosophy that I cobbled together myself over time. There it is. Simple. You proceed according to the type of client you have, little girl. Just like there are many types of whores. There are also many types of clients. There are those who just breeze through. They have nothing but this to do, in order not to say that they have plenty of things to do. They're people who seem very busy. But they can't resist it. A session between the sheets; that clears their minds. It helps to begin or end their day in all its beauty. They have this way of surprising you, of smacking your ass like you didn't expect it. As though smacking a whore's ass was something uncommon, something marvelous, so much so that they know how to do it better than anyone. It's all they've ever done their whole life. Smack whores' asses. These clients are among the ones who pay well, but who don't have enough time for caresses, for sucking or to be sucked off for their money. Surrounded by their security agents, they climb into new cars, windows tinted, that burn rubber as they peel out.

Everything began with a fall. One that gave me my freedom, at this exact moment when I decided to break the silence. It's been twelve years since then, if I remember correctly. It was raining hard on Grand Rue. The street was completely soaked, like usual. A little girl came knocking at my door to ask if I could let her stay the night. My name is Shakira. I have nowhere else to go, she told me, and I hate my mother. I don't want to live with her anymore. The rain kept me from distinguishing her tears. But her voice delivered the shock vigorously. I had pity on her.

I'd rather kill myself than go back home and live with my mother, she continued. It truly seemed like a ruse to convince me. But I didn't have a choice. You don't slam the door in peoples' faces like that. Not in the face of a girl like that, at any rate. Beautiful and undeniably audacious.

The clients. There are those who come for the first time, brought by a friend or by themselves. Sometimes, they're so timid that they seem scared. Especially if they're already in a committed relationship, married, fathers and everything. They'd rather take you somewhere else so that they don't get noticed by someone who could report their fugue to their wife. These clients, they gravitate toward the edge of social cliffs and have a habit of showing up during work hours. You see what I mean?

There are also those who don't move around at all. Offering their services voluntarily. We even came up with a name for them. *Tchyoul Bouzen*.\* Fucking dogs. There it is. Simple. The one who helps you find four blowjobs earns the right to one blowjob. Eight blowjobs, two blowjobs. Twelve blowjobs, the rest of the night. Little assholes who want to split without paying after coming, after having relieved themselves in a whore's mouth, the *Tchyoul Bouzen* hunt them down and beat the shit out them. Never start before you get paid.

---

\* *Chyoul Bouzen* refers to a pimp. In Haitian Creole, the word *chyoul* means pimp and the word *bouzen* refers to a sex worker or a prostitute.

Providing is the thing that I have never been good at doing, and this, despite my great generosity. I'm never satisfied with the circumstances, everything that revolves around my care. When forced to provide anyway, I provide poorly. Forgive me, little girl, if I never knew how to *provide well*.

Me and the other whores, we took on the habit of almost making love from time to time. Rubbing one another. Taking turns penetrating one another with dildos. Her, no. Except during the rare orgies, when we're hired out elsewhere, in the beautiful bourgeois neighborhoods for example, where everyone sucks, fucks, penetrates everyone and gets sucked, fucked, and penetrated by everyone simultaneously. I didn't see coming between us these feelings of filiation that I felt for quite some time. Since after the shooting on Grand Rue that killed my parents . . . so many parents. . . . It's a long story. I don't want to talk about it.

You've got to work at night and rest during the day, little girl. It's better at night. The cats are gray at night. The night is best for avoiding the clients' faces, their expressions at the moment when they ejaculate. You can spend all the nights in the world tricking in this city without anyone recognizing you. The night hides the true face of the world.

Here, take this bag. A whore without a bag is like a soldier without a uniform, without a gun. A whore should never be separated from her bag. Take it. You'll need it to put all your little things in. The money the clients throw at you. Everything. Your condoms. Your earrings. Your spare cloths. Your slutty clothing. All that a whore needs to shine. Me, I want you to shine. That you look like a real whore: an immortal.

The clients. Nothing but sons of bitches who run up the price higher and higher if they have to in order to possess you, to take more and more of you in every direction, to ask you to bark like a dog, to become a dog. To have it all. And afterwards leave the carcass to the dogs. Those who think that with their money they can eventually comprehend the immense infinity that is the heart of a woman.

You've got to work on your sex appeal, little girl. Cry, moan even before they touch you. The clients, they love that, you know. You have to give them the impression that their money wasn't worth nothing, that they're worth something. After serving a client, you have to assure yourself that he'll come back.

You can't even know, little girl, how advantageous that can seem, how dangerous it is for a whore to be appreciated, loved by her clients, for a slave to be cherished by her master. The only unity possible between the oppressor and the oppressed is in the very act of oppression. The oppressed suffers. The oppressor climaxes.

I was always motivated by the desire to be completely free, she confided in me, to live my life as I see it. And, for me, to be a whore is to be completely free. I want to become a whore. It wasn't convincing enough. Because we don't need to be whores to be completely free. And it's not because we are whores that we are completely free. It's obvious. It wasn't convincing enough. But it still struck me.

I told her what I'd told all the other girls before her.

"Your body, it's your only instrument, little girl."

That night, it continued to rain. The street emptied of passersby and of dogs. I talked with her about the street. About clients. About Géralda Huge-Tits, the mother of all the whores. About Fedna "The Blowjob Queen." About Emma. About the Red BMW Man.... The room was dark; I slid into the calm waters, recently unleashed from a story with a thousand and one voices when, all the sudden, I heard a sound. She had already fallen asleep. Poor little girl.

The things that last until the end of time, they usually start with a joke, a funny comment, then it becomes more serious, inevitable. It's obvious. In the beginning, I really thought it was a joke, one of those wisecracks that someone says in a serious tone of voice to better surprise those listening, simply a phase, that she didn't really want to be a whore, that it would quickly pass. But she didn't take long in learning how to sell herself, from the moment when she realized that a real whore never looks back, she takes it on completely. It was finished between she and her mother. She made her choice. A whore *for life*.

Just as I never stopped insisting the little girl, and all the other girls before her. My body has always been my only instrument, my only chance, the only way out. And I never really asked myself, not even a single time, if it was really this type of life that I wanted, if another life for me existed. I never wanted to end up like these women who aren't proud, who have little desire to do themselves harm, in looking back on the road that they traveled.

The street is of extreme importance in this profession, little girl. Because it's where everything is in play and is bound to lure in clients. You negotiate and you bring them here, to this room, since you'll inevitably need a place to do it in. And afterward, you return on the hunt. Don't become a house-whore. To me, a whore is like the work of a great painter. They're made to be exhibited. To be seen. To be a feast for the eyes.

In the beginning, the Red BMW Man was for me some kind of insurmountable barrier. Certain whores of Grand Rue talk about his member in praiseworthy terms. Others only see in it a handicap that makes him a filthy animal, a burdensome fuck. The first time that he undressed before me, I threw his money back in his face saying that my pussy was made for something normal. Not for a third leg. Not for a fifth appendage.

What is the meaning of life when it is deprived of everything that really matters? My life, from now on, no longer has rhythm. My life is empty. I'm ready to sacrifice it for my daughter. To find her again. She left because of me. I'm the one who is responsible. I hadn't learned how to hide my tears from her. Make it seem like everything was fine between me and her father. She knew everything. I know. And I kept playing my role of the mother who doesn't want her daughter to experience the same type of misery. I imposed everything on her. I gave her the order to take Jesus as her personal savior, to go to church every Sunday, and to pray every day before eating and every night before going to bed. I was so hard on her that I sometimes ask myself if I held her responsible for her father's latest escapades. Because everything was going fine before she came into this world. I no longer called her my daughter. I deprived her of everything, at least of what she loved most. . . . Today, I realize that I was wrong. Like us, children also have the right to choose what they want for themselves. It's what they believe that makes them happy.

I'm prepared to do anything to make my amends.

I spent months frequenting the Christianity Hotel, Brice's brothel, with the goal of finding my daughter. And there, there's no need to tell you that it's still the mother who's talking. You're the writer. You must be quite capable of appropriating all the voices that live inside me, because they're also your voices. To feel in the deepest reaches of yourself how much she was terrified by the idea that her daughter, her only daughter, become a prostitute, sell her flesh to live, to survive, give herself away to eat. To court this encounter with the owner of this brothel and, in the process, with one of his girls. To provoke her own suicide. There they are, your skills as a decent writer. I never liked the way that he looked at me, Brice. Men get this devilish look standing before women's round asses.

"Five minutes ago, a beautiful lady was drinking beside me. She told me that she worked as a prostitute from the age of twelve and that it'd been twelve years since she had seen her mother," a man told me asking for you know what in exchange for telling me where the young lady went. That was at Brice's. At the Christianity Hotel.

I later found out that this man who said to have seen my daughter was one of Brice's friends. Some type of literature professor to whom he had without a doubt given the secret, said things about me. Everyone who wanted a taste of my pussy pretended to know where my daughter was. I was a full-time puppet at Brice's, at the Christianity Hotel. I made quite a few fuck-ups in wanting to follow my daughter's trace. In refusing to miss a chance to find her.

Hold on. Please. Please. Hold on. You and me, it's been twelve years of us together, of little moments of eternity and of fissures. You can't abandon me just like this. Hold on, my whore. There's only you. It seems like it's a full-scale catastrophe. Hold on. These things happen. Help is on the way. They have to be prepared for this. Hold on. I know that it's dark below. Stuck between a thousand pieces of concrete. I know that you're terribly afraid. I know. I'm afraid too. Afraid that you'll let go, that you let me fall. Afraid that you'll leave me now. Hold on. All you have to do is wait for them to get here. It's nighttime already. And it's still shaking. Hold on. Still, it's been forever since I've heard the sound of help. But they'll come at some time or another. They're prepared for this. To swoop down and help those at risk of dying. It's been three days since they've been en route. They've been delayed. I know how thirsty you must be. But water, when it finds nothing inside you, that can kill you on the spot by stopping your heart. They're coming. Hold on, my little girl. My little Niña-Shakira. Five days, seven days, ten days. . . . It's been an eternity that they've been on the way. They're coming. Hold on. They're not far. They will come.

We were all moved that day in witnessing the ease with which she spoke of the marvelous realism of Jacques Stephen Alexis with this professor of literature who was a regular for about twelve years.

"I read *In the Flicker of an Eyelid* in one sitting," she told him in a half celebratory, half enchanted tone of voice. "In this book, we feel all of mankind's urges, the whole world's urges, pulsating."

They both agreed in saying that *In the Flicker of an Eyelid* is one of those rare books that would leave its mark on centuries of literature. But for me, I didn't understand a word of what they were chirping about.

Imagine for a moment that the sky is made of concrete. That *this thing* lasted an eternity. That the earth can no longer stop shaking. That the sun can never come up again. That we are the only people on earth.

The professor traveled frequently. The first thing to do when you arrive in a foreign city, he explained, is to find a brothel. A city without whores is a ghost town.

"When we wake up in the morning, we don't ask ourselves what book we're going to read. But rather what we're going to sink our teeth into. I suggest you close your Jacques Stephen whatever and get to work," I told her seriously, when she made me a part of her desire to quit hustling, to trick for some time to read.

Get that into your little whore brain, little girl. Never ask a client to be gentle with you. The day that you expose your Achilles heel, you'll be walked all over. It's just a nobody, a stranger who pays you for a service. The moment he sways you, he's your man. Make sure that he gets the maximum amount of pleasure, and you the maximum amount of money. You have no other guarantees. Another thing. Never try to surprise yourself by trying to refine the work with a client. Squabbling in the middle of the street over a wig, a bra, tights, nail polish, stolen perfume or whatever else. It's just simply a pain. Our stretch of dignity, it's worth fighting for, right?

I think I've told you just about everything, little girl. It's your play now. You have the lucky advantage of being very young. Of being new. The clients, they like that, fresh meat. They have their own way of expressing it.

—I just discovered uncharted territory.

The men and the other whores were always at the center of our discussions. And on that particular day, we were talking about this man traumatized by the disappearance of his wife, who he wants to find at all costs through all the women he meets. His problem, is that he perceives women as a kind of statue that must agree with everything he says and does. Even still, it's not because a statue doesn't move that makes her a statue; it's obvious. An hour later, the earth shook.

*The day crumbles*
*The night envelops everything*
*inert*
*fissured*
*time has lost all desire to move forward*
*each body is a pit which engulfs*
*all the cries of the earth*
*alone in the absolute darkness of night*
*a city agonizes*

Electrocuted. Crushed. Disintegrated. Besieged by an army of strange beings, made up in with an iconic mixture of dust, tears and blood flowing from everywhere and nowhere. The city resembled a theater of ghosts.

Close to a church, two dead among an infinity—one facing the other, their hands held firmly together, a man and a woman still wearing their wedding attire—laid out on a board. This time, nobody was capable of saying which, between life and death, was stronger.

On the ground floor of a collapsed house, an entire family started singing before giving away their souls. A song that spoke of the afterlife, of the heavens, of eternal rest . . .

*This thing* struck like it had stopped the heart of the city. Suddenly. It came with the night—the night had never been so long, dark and full of uncertainty—and this night burst with screams. Lots of screaming. All sorts of screaming. When will we wake up from this terrible nightmare?

I don't like to talk. It's not that it's a bad thing. But to me, it's annoying. Especially if it's a discussion about something that I know nothing about. As soon as the professor arrives, I leave or I ask the little girl to leave. Not only does it annoy me that he calls her "My Niña Estrellita," but the two only talk about literature. About fiction. My time is too limited for this type of exercise, this type of gratuitous game. There are clients who tell me constantly. Business first. I don't have time to waste.

Yes. I remember saying that sometimes it happens that men and the other whores are at the center of our discussions. All that I can say for the time being is that women are not always in the best position to talk about men. Neither are whores to talk about other whores. I don't know; there's always an unavoidable element of injustice and hypocrisy when we talk about others.

No, I don't want to forget. I must tell it, this never-before-seen story of a brief phenomenon. I must tell you, my own little Niña-Shakira. So that I stop wasting time thinking about the banality of life. About the debris of tragedy. About things that we took an entire life to build and that disappear in less than a minute. In the flicker of an eyelid. We must move on.

Can you give me a cigarette, writer? We're going to take a break. Take advantage of the time to correct what we've already laid out on paper. I hope I can continue tomorrow or the day after. If my heart allows me.

Tell me how to get there all alone. Without you by my side. Without anyone to tell me off from time to time. Tell me. Tell me how to live with the idea that you are no more. Tell me how to fill the void that you've left behind. Tell me how you could keep it from me for so long, that you had a son somewhere. You dirty little ingrate. I opened my heart and home to you. You lied to me. You lied from the very beginning. You let yourself be entertained by this impostor of a shitty professor. He got you pregnant. And you did nothing. You said nothing. You who never saw yourself as a little slut. I trusted you. You dishonored me. As well as all the other immortals of Grand Rue. How? How could you do that to me, me? Tell me how to forever erase you from my memory. Dirty liar. I hate you. Dirty little whore. I should've never met you. You would've been dead a long time ago. Yes, a long time ago.

The little girl. She had everything to succeed. I missed the chance to help her become a good person. Like her mother hoped. To be a mother to her. Without asking anything from her in return. That's what I mean by *providing well.*

When she came knocking at my door, I was getting ridden by the Red BMW Man. He really loved fucking when it rained. Or I was putting the containers under the holey parts of the canvas ceiling in my room. Or I was getting ready to get in bed to be cradled by the soft music of the falling rain on the roof. I no longer remember certain things, lots of things. How much longer do I have left to live with this fissured memory? I softly opened the door, with the fear of coming across one of those highway robbers that waits around every hour of the day, only to come across this beautiful phenomenon.

Is there any pride in being a whore? Let's take the example of Géralda Huge-Tits. *Gwo manman bouzen* for all eternity. The mother of all whores. The spiritual mother for all us whores. It's true that she built two-room homes and schooled her *kaka-san-savon* in the profession—for a whore, this happens once for every thousand—but why, like mine, were her eyes always so sad, did she always find so many reasons to lower them? A *kaka-san-savon* is a child born to an unknown father.

Géralda Huge-Tits. She always wore an amulet around her neck, high-quality earrings, and bracelets that made her forearms almost invisible. Wasted her time talking about the supernatural, things from another world, which escape our understanding. . . . Those versed in the art of gossip say that she inherited a *lwa* from her mother, and it's this *lwa* that made her a whore. She had a madras that she placed over the head of her clients to make them walk, salivate like dogs. Every year, she went to one of those far-flung corners, outside of the capital, to prepare the reception of and the *manje ranje* given to these spirits, the traces of which and where they are treated to these offerings are never to be seen. A *lwa* is a Vodou spirit.

Don't forget, little girl. You're a whore. And real whores never let go like that. A whore must hold on tight. You have to hold on tight, my little girl. My own little Niña-Shakira. They're coming. Maybe their cars broke down or they're stuck in traffic jams. I'm afraid they also need help. Or, like you, they're stuck under the rubble. Or dead, crushed by one of these big buildings. But, they'll come. Hold on. I never asked anything of you. All I ask is for you to hold on tight. I know that you can do it. They're coming. They're on their way to get you out of there, my little girl. My little Niña-Shakira. Hold on. Shit. No. You can't do this to me. It's not right. No. What are you saying, these silly things? These confessions. These violent hiccups. Are you there? Are you there? Talk to me! Please, talk to me! Talk to me, I'm begging you! I'm begging you! talk . . .

Before, to be a mother for me meant to deploy my labor. To no longer be totally, absolutely free. To be a slave of my own stupidity. I was happy enough to be a whore and it suited me well. Since it was my world, my profession. Now, I see things completely differently since that night when she came knocking at my door. I became aware of my ability to listen beyond the silence of others and to see beyond their sight.

I didn't like to see her suffer, the little girl. To spend an entire day reading after having dedicated her entire evening to being pulled every which way, sucking, relieving tons of randoms. These fucking books kept her from taking care of herself, from looking like a whore, from participating in the jokes amongst friends. If I could, I would tear them apart one by one, page by page, in a thousand pieces. I told her from the beginning.

—Your body is your only instrument, little girl.

Géralda Huge-Tits. She wasn't a simple woman. Everyone knew that. Shouldn't fuck around with her, if so she'd immediately set out for one of those far-flung corners, outside of the capital. And even before she got back, you're already tricking with the dead, six feet under. Every evening before going out to prowl the streets, she took baths in rare leaves, giving her a strong scent and allowing her to be assailed by men fighting with one another to be the first one to taste her pussy, right there, under the jealous gaze of the others. The monster's joists gave way. She died with a client's head between her thighs.

Without wanting to interfere too much with the direction of your work, writer, I'd like for you to add this notebook to your story. I found it in her bag a few days before the drama. It's without a doubt hers. I recognize her handwriting.

*I hate my mother. Just the thought of being her daughter makes me hate myself even more. The fruit of her entrails. My mother. She played her maternal role so well. But I don't love her. I never loved her. I will never love her. To be a mother, for me, it's bullshit. We can't choose who we are. We have the right to love our mother or not, right?*

*My mother. She's ready for everything. The most unthinkable of sacrifices as long as it will make me happy. I never saw somebody in all my life be so courageous, and inflexible. . . . All that she cares about is my well-being. She never stops telling me that; each time it's under the guise of a reprimand.*

*My mother. She loves me with a boundless love. Like a mother loves her child. She's all that I have. But I don't love her. I really tried. I just can't.*

The little girl. She closed her ears to all my never-ending reproaches. She refused to wash her sheets. Did weird things. Anyway, things that whores don't normally do. The books that she read greatly impacted the way she thought, the way she saw the world. Everything was bullshit to her. The world is bullshit. Humans are bullshit. Everything Géralda Huge-Tits said about the spirits, the supernatural ..."There's something much stronger than these minute little treatments," the strange woman said. "All these artifices of seduction whores can't get enough of. All this relentless fighting to stay young. Something more profound than makeup. A flat stomach. Fuck me lips. Shoes with heels that look like perroquet beaks. Watermelon-sized breasts. Breathtaking curves. An ass just like that, which makes everyone turn their heads to the point where they leave with a stiff neck. Little lace panties that gives a preview of your pussy, that gives men a hard-on in two or three movements, or ejaculate like a faucet, all that's left to imagine themselves in the right place. Something mysterious, unattainable. To which only the *lwa* hold the secret. That makes the client choose one whore and let go of the rest. That draws them in ..." The little girl. She said that all that, it's bullshit. Freedom is the only god she knows.

The little girl. She was always opposed to theories that imply that everything is related to a mystical cause. A whore is a whore, she said, because it suits her to receive clients who pay her for her services. Point fucking blank.

I told her that literature wasn't something for people like us, for whores. To leave that to people who have nothing better to do. The fortunate. Those who have rights. Maybe I was wrong.

Géralda Huge-Tits was a house whore. House whore, meaning in-home service. A hole without any other occupation than to take in from all sides at least twelve clients per day, in a cramped room that reeks of sperm and death. Where there was only, among its decorations, a chamber pot, a wooden bed made of oak, a dirty and cracked mirror that only reflected a few scraps of an image or a completely deformed image, and a few accessories for whores. A decor that left nothing for other whore's chambers to desire. But one day, just like that, to everyone's great surprise, she decided to post on the sidewalk. She told herself quite simply, to better convince herself, that the stay-at-home attitude of certain whores was due to a refusal, a lack of self-confidence. She no longer wanted to be a house whore. It's strange. A Géralda Huge-Tits who never opted for the street, now she puffed out her chest like a peacock. We couldn't believe it. . . . It's what the *lwa* desire, what God desires.

In trying to boycott her relationship with this pretentious literature professor who will not stop calling her "My Niña-Estrellita"—the other clients, convinced that it had something to do with the Colombian star, that she could also swing her hips around at twenty thousand miles per hour, giving you vertigo, and make you see January before December, called her Shakira—brought her new books with each visit. *The 120 Days of Sodom*. *The Elementary Particles*. *The Immortals*, and many others; I thought it was a good thing, but it only made the situation worse.

"Don't forget it. It's with our chests that we pay the rent around here. Us, we don't have time to fall in love. Love is for other people. This man, not only is he ugly and cynical, but he's thirty-six years older than you. You have to respect the rules of the game. You're a whore, in case you might have forgotten."

*I loathe everyone who thinks that the mother is the greatest source of wealth a child can have. It's bullshit. You don't need a mother in order to follow your dreams. All you need is yourself, completely. I think that I would live a better life if my mother were already dead, buried.*

*My hatred is infinite. Because it grows day by day and stretches toward eternity. How can one come to hate their own mother to such an extent? One who, when everyone asks you to split, waits with both arms wide open.*

That night, it was brusque and quick. If only it left you the time to escape. How do you expect me, writer, to understand that? Destiny wanted you to be here today, in this room, in front of me, in the exact spot where she liked to sit and read, for you to witness everything. For you to make her living among the dead. The little girl. She said it frequently. The characters in books never die. They're the masters of time.

How to put it? How to find the words to express her love for books? These objects, she said, that take up little space in the house, but occupy a lot of space inside of you, in your heart, they shed light on the deepest depths, the darkest reaches of yourself.

The little girl. She loved books with a crazy kind of love. A kind of love never seen before. . . . Bah! A whore who reads. Always interested in the grand debates. In everything written by a ton of crusty folks she calls the *literary masters* and who give themselves up to Shakira!

We'll have seen everything!

The little girl. She refused to wash her sheets. I already said that. Caught in a nervous breakdown, I threatened to throw her and her books, strewn about the room, out the door if she didn't find a place, at this instant, to put them. But she didn't let me. She wouldn't have let me do it. She had left and came back a year later.

She had everything to succeed. Beauty and audacity. Travel was her only solace. A year without even a word from her. A year of silence. A year to covet her treasure. I have never suffered so much someone else's absence. She left because of me, because I threatened to throw her out the door with her books. Because I understood nothing, I did nothing to keep her here.

*My mother. Nobody can replace her. Because I'll never come to hate anyone as much as I hate her now. She always takes my age—twelve— as a pretext to doubt my ability to do anything. I see the day coming when I'll take care of myself. I'll leave home for good. And I'll do what I want for myself.*

*She does everything to please the man who treats her like garbage, who takes himself for the only living god. My mother, she makes me want to vomit. I can't stand anymore to see her beg for him not to break up with her, to not slap her so hard that the neighbors don't hear her crying. Shakira is the name I would have chosen to break with all this, with the tears that she never manages to hide from me. It will be my name, my name in exile, in constant flight . . .*

There's an *i* that I would like to dot. The little girl. She only wanted another name. A name that isn't her real one, a name that isn't hers. A name-cave in which she could hide. Far from the past. Far from her mother. She chose Shakira. Just like that. Without thinking twice. Or just because it almost sounds like "qué sera." Whatever happens, she said every time to the beautiful young girl with sad eyes standing in the mirror undressing for a client. As it concerns the looks of the real Shakira. . . . She was kind of lukewarm on the subject. Her hair in a bizarre disorder. Her svelte body. Her manner of being on stage, of moving her hips. Her pirouettes. All that fascinated her, the little girl. She said that she'd make a good whore, the real Shakira. But not to the point of imitating her. Of making her a role model. Far from that. The idea of becoming someone else had never occurred to her to. Neither god nor master. She wanted to look like no one.

*I read, I write not to hear my parents arguing. To be far away from my mother's tears. Far from the sound of the smacks she receives from her man. To open myself to the world, to the wind, to new horizons. To live on the other side of the abyss and of time.*

*People will always find it senseless, and baseless, my hatred for my mother. But I don't have to justify it either. I said it, you can't choose the way you are. Nothing can fill the void between us. We're not the same. We never will be. All that she ever wants, my mother, all she ever wanted, was to be the prisoner, the doormat of this man who treats her like the thing he wipes his ass with. And me, all that I would like, all that I've ever wanted, was to find myself on an infinite highway on a moving bus, moving with the sea that marches before my eyes without the slightest chance that it'll stop one day.*

The little girl. After her fugue, she no longer talked about Jacques Stephen Alexis, even less about the professor. Done with books. Done with the grand debates and the habit she had of jerking him off, blowing him in the backseat of his car. Spending time with him on the phone about things I'll never know about. Although, she had told me that the relationship between her and this man never surpassed the threshold of literature and taxable pleasure. I asked her nothing more either. If there is one thing she taught me, it's to respect the private life of others.

Who was she with? Where was she? What was she doing during this long absence? After she left, I never stopped asking myself questions and inventing scenarios. I was suspicious of this literature professor from the day that he set foot in here and paid up-front for twelve months in a row. A professor who grovels all the livelong day in brothels, where does he find the time to teach his classes?

The little girl. She never told me her real name. And me, I was happy to call her Shakira. The first thing that she told me that night on the footstep of my door. Shakira, my name is Shakira. So, I simply continued to call her that. Like it was nothing. Like I had heard everyone call her from the day she made her way down to my place. Shakira, the new whore of Grand Rue. Look, it's Shakira, the daughter of the woman who sells bibles and books of Gospel songs!

I imagine that she has a name that evokes elsewhere. A name that refers to death. A name that's more than a real name. No, I never asked her, for her real name. Best not to know, to reinforce the symbol of clandestinity that she always thought she was. To better drown out the past. The mother's image.

*My mother. I don't love her. I'll never stop repeating it. She never did any-thing for me to hate her to such an extent. What kind of mother is capable of hurting her child? To what can we compare a mother's love, a mother's courage? I just don't love her. That's it.*

*That night, I had a dream. And in my dream, my father got up one morning and left home for good. Never showing his face again.*

*My father. I know he slapped her around. That he only saw in my mother a staid woman. This zonbi woman. Made to look after the house and her daughter. Made to hide her eyes, her nest of tears, that always looked elsewhere. Always far away. To where he became once again this exemplary man who respects and takes care of his wife. Who whispers in her ear from time to time little "I love you's" followed by little kisses on her neck, and all the shit that, in time, no longer mean a thing. To where she no longer knew the misery of this fucking "for better or worse" that transformed her life into a living hell . . .*

*My mother. She had no problem crying all the tears in her body in the arms of her little six-year-old daughter—me—when her man, one morning, like in my dream, set sail forever. Never to show his face again.*

After her fugue, everything began to look different. Clients became scarce. The room was no longer this well where they came to drown their sorrows, their fears. I was completely powerless. I no longer had any influence on her. All I did was plead with her in the dark. Suffering in the silence of her silence. In her increasingly pale reality, more and more deprived of light. Her decline. A trapped animal who sees death on the horizon. She who used to be the most coquettish. The most coveted of the streets. For clients who devoured one another to kiss at her feet, her thighs, her eyes . . .

The Christianity Hotel is one of the rare Grand Rue brothels where you could find beer in short-sleeves. The beer is so frozen that it becomes white like it's wearing a white short-sleeve shirt. I've never been there myself. Not one single time. The little girl, yes, with the professor. There are many rumors that go around about this place. The police come in from time to time and leave with guys bound up that they shove toward the car. Brice and the professor are old friends, childhood friends, I said so once before, I think. They loved to whisper little things in each other's ear and broke out in big bursts of laughter afterward.

The points of convergence and divergence between me and her mother. Her mother and I, we both loved her with all our hearts. Neither she nor I could prevent her from identifying with the world, with her sorrow. With this Jacques Stephen Alexis. With this pile of gobbledygook written by crazy do-nothings. Brice fucked her mother twelve times. The BMW Man fucked me twelve times. I lived on Grand Rue. Her mother in Martissant. I'm a peddler of joy. Her mother is a peddler of bibles and Gospel songs. I'm a whore. Her mother is a whore disguised as a Christian. She broke all the ties between she and her mother. Between she and I, too, but after a year, came back, to me.

Her mother. She wanted her to become a Christian like herself. I hate Christians. They believe that on judgment day that they'll live in the heavens with God in a crystal palace reserved for those who observed the Ten Commandments to the letter. And the image that they have of this God, is that he is so Godly that he could at once resolve all the world's problems and bring about its end. It's the God of the beginning and the end of time. The past, present, and future. When you're a whore, you're a whore. Being a Christian means nothing. There are too many impostors in the world. All that she dreamed of, the little girl—she never partook in any big litany, not calling on the benevolence of any sort of divinity—was of finding her treasure, one day, and taking him into her arms.

I acted without thinking. Without seeing what I walked into, that evening Brice took me into his bedroom. I jumped at the opportunity, like someone who was waiting for it all their life. I also forgot that I was a Christian, and that a Christian does not have the right to fornicate, to have sex outside of marriage. I didn't have a choice. After all these years, all the signs were right for finding my daughter. I never saw coming against me this general resistance from the others. To be completely frank, I never even thought of it.

"Where does she get off, this granny, this Model T Ford who came along and stole our dear Brice from us, huh? Get fixed up somewhere else, bitch! Go get fucked somewhere else!"

*Come. Take my clothes off. Rip me apart. Fuck me hard. Find my mother inside me. Do everything to her. Give it all to her. Be rougher. I want her to be a whore, a slut, my mother. For her to come.*

*As long as I'm her daughter and her this man's wife, I'll never find freedom and she'll never be my mother.*

*For me, there exist two great journeys. Reading and the sumptuous shipwreck of entangled bodies. I love freedom too much. I have too many fantasies. I thirst for elsewhere, to remain this little mommy's girl who receives dolls for Christmas. This cherished little girl, cared for, who can't move one degree without brushing up against the barrier of maternal protection. I want for my body to exult. To be the chest that shimmers like the stars.*

Aye, Brice! Go slowly. Give it to me, do anything you want with me. But don't smack my ass. You know very well that I'm a Christian woman looking for her daughter. Not so hard. Go slowly. The wages of sin is death, Brice. Aye! That's it, Brice. That's it. May God bless you, Brice. May he bless you. For taking me so high, to the heavens. No, no spanking. I'm a Christian woman. Not so hard. Give it to me. Give me it all. Aye! Shit, that's it. That's so good. Shit. Smack my ass. Spank me, Brice. Hit me. Kill me. Your name? Say your name? Yes. Yes, Papa Brice. Dear Papa Brice. Yes. May he bless you. Shit. Kill me, shit. That's it . . . Yes . . .

Christianity Hotel. It's what I could call the somber page in my life. Brice is a dirty profiteer. A good for nothing. Each time, it's the same tune.

"I'm going to help you find her, your daughter, don't worry."

When he wriggles on top of me, my eyes plastered to the ceiling ruminating on the brief joys of childhood.

*In my dreams, I often see myself on this street. This street that cuts the city in two. This street buried in its noise, its contradictions, its own escapes. Between my parents' incessant arguing and the Niña-Estrellita's eyes. The dogs tickle the cadavers. "That tickles!" said the cadavers, bursting with laughter. This street whose lights have been out for ages, where I no longer bear my name, where I am no longer myself, no longer the same, the fragile little girl, privileged, who must be protected, looked after so that she doesn't see the street, because the street doesn't leave anyone indifferent, but Shakira the whore, the most beautiful, the most coveted, the most coquettish in the world. This street where clients, lunatics, and the possessed devour one another to kiss at my feet, my thighs, my eyes. . . . Me, Shakira, the whorest whore in the world.*

I was hopeless, tired of looking everywhere for her for all these years. I prepared to kill myself for good this time. And there, I won't go into details. Explain how I'm going to take myself out. I'm not writing a novel. It's without importance. I was going to put an end to everything when someone came to tell me that they saw her, my daughter, on Grand Rue, in a brothel with the name of the Christianity Hotel, in the company of a man who could've been her father . . .

I want for the Christianity Hotel to be from now on the last fuck-up of my life, thrown in the dustbin of my memory. The chances my daughter is still alive after *this thing* are minimal. I must resign myself to it at all costs. Resign myself. Here, this is what I was afraid of. And that's it. I'm going to think about killing myself again, to put an end to it all. There isn't a single day in these last twelve years when I haven't thought about killing myself.

Contrary to many others, I refuse to be a prodigal child. Almost all stories like this end the same way, they're all pitiful. They go back home to be reunited with those they left for an indeterminate amount of time. When I will have left my mother's house, I will never go back.

My mother. Why doesn't she kill herself or kill my father? To stop being his bitch, his victim. She is the perfect example of the animosity between men and women. For that, I'd love her with unrivaled affection. For once in her life having made a decision, accomplished something so noble. . . . The greatest religion of all is to come and go as you please, without having to be accountable to anyone. Freedom.

Brice. I don't want to listen to him anymore, the son of a bitch. I'm going to help you find your daughter, don't worry. These words kill me little by little. They rot my soul. I've had enough of being taken advantage of. Of letting him take me from the back door, in every direction. To be forced to do cocaine. To smoke tons of joints and such. Just for him to help me find my daughter. A Christian woman prays. Has faith. Everything that is impossible for man is possible for God. . . . But alas, it's already been some time since I've stopped being a Christian woman, this exemplary servant who announces the word of God wherever she goes, frequenting the brothels of Grand Rue, looking for my daughter.

Now it's over. Nothing more is possible. Everyone seems to be tired of playing with me. First Brice. I noticed it in his new way of looking at me. Unlike before, now he takes me in his arms to console me when I'm sad. When I cry.

*It's tonight when it's going to happen. I don't know how. But it'll happen. I'm going to leave my mother's house. Break this original bond that seems to forge us together forever. There is no worse torture than being loved by someone you detest and who will never be ready to give you reciprocity, whatever happens. To be the daughter of the type of Christian who puts everything on the count of faith. Who sees in everything the fulfillment of a prophecy, even the beatings her man gives her.*

Something had to be said, anything, in order not to slip into panic. A deadly attack that would've blown my brains out. It's not yet the end of the story. But we must stop here. However, I would like to thank you, writer, for agreeing to write it down while I told it. I know that I've been so silly, getting up from time to time to go piss, cry, to blow my nose or redo my makeup— you know, a whore's old habits—but most of all for sometimes encroaching, in an almost mean way, on your artistic freedom. With regard to the story itself, I was the one who chose to write it as such, drop by drop, without pedantry, with an almost revolting simplicity. The manuscript, you do with it what you want. I have a treasure to find. The thing that was the dearest to her in her whole fucking life. Wish me good luck.

You're the writer. You must be quite capable of appropriating all the voices that live inside me, because they're also
your voices.

First published in Montreal in 2010 by Mémoire d'encrier, *Les
Immortelles* (*The Immortals*) is both Orcel's debut novel and one of
the first works of fiction to discuss the January 12, 2010, earthquake that struck Port-au-Prince, Haiti, and its wake. One year
later, the novel was published in France by the Éditions Zulma
and was met with critical acclaim, winning the 2012 Prix Thyde
Monnier (Thyde Monnier Award) given to new and talented
writers in French. Orcel has followed *The Immortals* with four
additional novels: *Les Latrines* (2011), the multiple award-win-
ning *L'Ombre animale* (2016), and *Maître minuit* (2018), as well as
a collaborative text with Nicolas Idier, *Une boîte de nuit à Calcutta*
(2019). Translating Orcel's text into English has meant not only
trying to counter the forces that shape which stories we do and
don't hear about Haiti but also giving readers access to a much
broader literary tradition from Haiti and the Caribbean.

At the center of *The Immortals* is the story of Shakira, a girl
seeking freedom from her mother, dogmatic evangelism, and the
intricacies of her lived reality through literature. For Shakira,
reading is an escape. She falls in love with a novel called *L'Espace
d'un cillement* (*In the Flicker of an Eyelid*) by Jacques Stephen Alexis

about a self-aware young female Haitian Cuban sex worker nicknamed La Niña Estrellita. Although it is tempting to read Shakira as the latter's mirror image, she is perhaps more like another character in Alexis's novel, a Cuban woman named La Rubia who works with La Niña. Inspired after reading the seventeenth-century Mexican poet Sor Juana Inés de la Cruz by candlelight, La Rubia decides to begin writing as well, surreptitiously penning her own story by hand. Unlike La Rubia and Shakira, the primary female narrator of *The Immortals* is not a reader or writer per se. Nevertheless, the narrator indirectly learns from Shakira that stories can be passed on, immortalized even, through the written word—a lesson she follows in demanding that the writer "appropriate[e] all the voices that live inside me."

Of the many parts of *The Immortals* that I could quote in this afterword, I chose the epigraph because it reminds readers that Shakira's story and all the stories in Orcel's novel are in the hands of many people, including my own. In this passage, the unnamed female narrator interrupts the writer to remind him that his job is to write the story while she does the telling. Her reminder is particularly significant given the gender difference between them. *The Immortals* is a book written by a man, about a man writing, and translated into English by a man. Yet the novel is populated with women's voices, their kinship and their shared intimacies. The narrator, her protégé Shakira, and their neighbors are sex workers, living and working on Grand Rue, the busiest street in Port-au-Prince, when the earthquake strikes. Their stories are ones that often make readers in and beyond Haiti uncomfortable and which are routinely ignored or devalued, even as Haitian writers such as Alexis and Kettly Mars make them their focus. *The Immortals* asks us to sit with these stories, invites us to walk down Grand Rue and bear witness to the lives that Haitian sex workers lived in the days before the brothels fell.

In Orcel's writing, the lives of these women cannot be reduced to a moralizing or romanticizing tale of prostitution such as we find in works by Charles Baudelaire (whose name also appears in these pages), Walt Whitman, Émile Zola, or Gabriel García Márquez. The women in *The Immortals* are individuals with hobbies, habits, and obsessions, who deserve to have their stories told. Shakira has her love for books and things of this world, including her relationship with the narrator. We see their love and care for one another as well as their arguments and trivial gripes. Fedna adores the television. It is her window onto a world that is not her own—an infinity of telenovelas and gameshows to which she escapes when her clients leave. Geralda finds safety and solace in the sacred art of Vodou. Her religious practice brings her the confidence to walk through the world with her head held high. *The Immortals* imagines a world where these women can live and die without losing their right to human dignity.

To translate this novel into English is my attempt, albeit modest, to provide stories of Haitians that audaciously defy the stories we tell in the United States about Haitians. More than a decade after the quake, this work, like the work of translation itself, is an ongoing process.

NATHAN H. DIZE
*Nashville, Tennessee*

# ABOUT THE AUTHOR

Born in Port-au-Prince in 1983, Makenzy Orcel is the author of four highly acclaimed novels and numerous collections of poetry published in Haiti, Canada, and France. *The Immortals* is his first novel, originally published as *Les Immortelles* in Montreal, Canada (2010), and later in France (2012). Orcel's latest novels are *Maître minuit* (2018) and *Une boîte de nuit* à Calcutta (2019), which he coauthored with the French writer Nicolas Idier.